Belles

Bella

This series is for my riding friend
Shelley, who cares about all animals.

STRIPES PUBLISHING
An imprint of Magi Publications
1 The Coda Centre, 189 Munster Road, London SW6 6AW

A paperback original
First published in Great Britain in 2007

Text copyright © Jenny Oldfield, 2007
Illustrations copyright © Sharon Rentta, 2007
Cover illustration © Simon Mendez, 2007

ISBN-13: 978-1-84715-025-7

A CIP catalogue record for this book is available from the British Library.

Printed and bound in Belgium by Proost

2 4 6 8 10 9 7 5 3 1

Bella

Tina Nolan
Illustrated by Sharon Rentta

stripes

ANIMAL MAGIC
Meet the animals

Visit our website at
www.animalmagicrescue.net

Working our magic to match the perfect pet with the perfect owner!

FRANKIE
A lively young ferret who had a bad start in life. Frankie is now looking for a fun-loving, kind owner. Are you that person?

SASHA
A Labrador and Border collie cross, 6 weeks old. Email us fast or she'll be gone!

BILLY
This lively 2-year-old boxer is bored! He needs more long walks and lots of TLC.

RESCUE CENTRE
in need of a home!

ELLIE
How can anyone not love Ellie? She's a gentle, sweet-tempered German shepherd who never loses her cool.

JIMMY
This little guinea pig's twinkling eyes will win you over and you'll long to take him home. Just look at his picture and fall in love!

LUCKY
A gorgeous black and white Dutch rabbit who is lonely and looking for a friend.

MISSY AND PETAL
Sisters who would love to stay together. Can you offer these adorable tabby kittens a home?

Chapter One

"But this is a puppy. She's a living breathing creature – not a machine!" Heidi Harrison told the woman in Reception at Animal Magic.

The visitor had marched in a few minutes earlier carrying a cardboard box containing a tiny black puppy.

Eva sat at the computer, surprised by her mum's angry tone.

"They told me at the place where I bought her that this puppy was house-trained," the woman complained in a whining voice. "But when I got her home, she started leaving puddles everywhere!"

"That's because Sasha is only about six weeks old," Heidi explained more patiently. "It's much too soon for her to be house-trained."

The woman frowned. She was fashionably dressed in a short skirt and pink flowered top. "They also told me that she slept through the night and that she'd be perfectly happy to be left at home during the day while I go out to work. But it's not true."

"You leave Sasha by herself *all* day?" Heidi raised her eyebrows. She glanced at Eva, who pulled a face as she tapped at the keyboard to update the Animal Magic website.

I don't believe it! Eva thought darkly.

Some people don't deserve pets!

Her mum took a deep breath. "OK, let me get this straight. The breeders told you that Sasha was a pure-bred Labrador, whereas in fact she's a cross-breed – a mix of Labrador and collie by the look of it."

Eva turned to see the puppy raise her cute head over the top of the box and let out a faint whimper. *Poor little thing!*

"Plus, she's not house-trained. Plus she cries all night long?" Heidi added.

The woman nodded three times. "So I don't want to keep her," she said firmly. "That's why I brought her here. After all, you are a rescue centre, aren't you?"

"Cross-breeds are often very good-natured," Heidi said quietly. "They can make better pets than pedigree dogs."

Definitely! Eva thought. *No way are cross-breeds second best!* But it was clear her mum was losing the argument.

"So will you take her, or not?" the woman asked, tapping the side of the box and glancing at her watch.

Sasha whined and scrabbled with her paws.

Heidi succeeded in hiding her irritation. "Sure," she said brightly. "She's a gorgeous little thing. It shouldn't take us long to find her a suitable new home."

Better than the one you gave her, Eva thought, glaring at the woman's pink, flowery back as she turned to leave. Some people needed a big reality check before they rushed out and bought a pet!

As Heidi showed the woman to the door, Eva came over and lifted the puppy out of the box and put her gently on the desk. "Hey, Sasha, she didn't even say goodbye to you, did she?" she murmured.

Sasha squirmed and yelped, weeing in panic as her paws slipped on the smooth surface.

"Oops!" Eva smiled, lifting her carefully and cuddling her. "You're gorgeous!" she murmured as the puppy snuggled close. Soft and silky, with big brown eyes and floppy ears, and a little pointed tail that wagged to and fro.

"It makes me so cross when people dump their pets as if they were dropping off a bundle of old clothes at a charity shop!" Heidi sighed, coming back into Reception. "I'm also worried about that breeder passing off cross-breeds as pure pedigrees. I think it's worth following up."

Eva nodded as Sasha licked her hand. "You're totally gorgeous!" she sighed. "You'll be snapped up the minute we put you up on our website – just wait and see!"

"Eva's in lurve!" Karl chanted. "She lurves the new puppy 'cos she's so cute and fluffy!"

"Who's cute and fluffy – Eva or the dog?" Eva and Karl's dad asked, poking his head into Reception. Mark Harrison had just got home from a sunny day delivering parcels. He was in a good mood, ready to tease his daughter. "Or both?" he suggested.

Eva ignored the joke and carried on tidying leaflets in the rack. "We admitted a new puppy called Sasha," she told him. "Karl just took her picture and put her on the website."

"L-U-R-V-E – lurve!" Karl laughed, unhooking a dog lead and going to fetch Billy the boxer from the kennels.

"I'm taking Billy for a walk by the river," he told them.

The boxer jumped up when he saw Karl's lead, wagging his stump of a tail.

"Down!" Karl ordered. "Sit, Billy!"

The lean brown dog did as he was told.

"Good boy." Karl clipped on the lead and took Billy off across the yard.

"Nice dog," Mark said. "Pity about his habit of chewing people's shoes to shreds."

"And chair legs and tables," Eva reminded him. "But it's not Billy's fault. His owner used to lock him in a room and he was bored."

Billy was a chewer and it had landed him at Animal Magic and in need of a new home. So far they'd had two sets of people come to look at the lively two year old, but both had turned him down because of his bad habit.

"Hi, Eva. Hi, Mr Harrison!" Annie Brooks said as she breezed in. Eva's friend from next door had come to see the puppy that Eva had called to tell her about. "So where's this cute pup?"

"In the kennels. Come on!" Leaving the leaflets, Eva dashed ahead. "Sasha's mega sweet, Annie. Honestly, you just have to take a peep!"

"Karl's out walking Billy, and Eva's in the kennels with Annie," Mark reported to Heidi, who had just finished talking with Joel, Animal Magic's veterinary assistant.

"Did Annie bring any news?" Heidi asked. "You know, from Linda – about the Council's decision."

For more than a week now they'd been

waiting nervously for a letter from the Council.

"No news I'm afraid." Mark shook his head. "I only know that Linda wishes she'd never got up that petition to have us closed down in the first place."

Heidi frowned. "Yes, well, a dose of guilt won't do Linda Brooks any harm. Meanwhile, we're living on tenterhooks, wondering whether we're going to be shut down."

Mark put an arm around her shoulder. "Fingers crossed they let us stay open," he said. "Anyway, forget that now, come and see what's in the van!"

"Hey, go and see who we've got in Reception!" Karl told Eva and Annie.

The two girls had spent half an hour

cuddling and petting lonely little Sasha. Karl was back from his walk and putting Billy in his kennel.

"Who?" Eva demanded. It was early evening – a busy time for Animal Magic.

"Put that puppy down and go see!" Karl insisted.

"Just because you want to cuddle Sasha!" Eva grinned.

"Yeah, Karl!" Annie joined in. "You won't admit it, but really you do!"

"OK then, don't go!" he sulked. "But you're missing something interesting."

"Here!" Eva said, making up her mind and handing Sasha to him. "Watch she doesn't wee all over you!"

Out in Reception, Joel and Eva's mum and dad were gathered around a low table in the waiting area.

"Who's a cheeky boy?" a croaky voice asked. "Who's a cheeky boy?"

"What's that?" Annie gasped, tumbling through the door with Eva.

"Where's Neville? Who's a cheeky boy?" *Chirp-chirp-croak!*

"It's a bird," Eva decided, though she couldn't see clearly.

Mark leaned close to the cage and made little kissing noises. Joel's broad back hid the occupant from sight.

"Is it a parrot?" Annie asked.

"Cage is too small," Eva muttered.

"Bud-dy! Bud-dy!" the voice croaked. "Who's a cheeky boy?"

Heidi stood back to let Eva and Annie see. "Meet Buddy the budgie," she said with a smile.

Inside the cage was a small, sky-blue bird with a white head and a grey freckled ruff of feathers around his neck. He hopped up and down on his little perch, bobbing his head and repeating his favourite phrase.

"Aah!" Annie said with a sigh. "He's cute!"

The budgie hopped from one perch to another, jingling a tiny silver bell above his head. "Who's a cheeky boy?" he cried, cocking his head to one side.

Eva crouched by the cage. She gazed into Buddy's button-black eyes. "Cool!" she murmured.

Buddy stared back at her without blinking. "Where's Neville?" he croaked. "Poppety-poppety-poppety-pop!"

Chapter Two

"Who's Neville?" Eva asked her dad the following morning.

Buddy the budgie had been going on about Neville ever since he arrived.

"Neville is Buddy's owner," Mark explained. "He's left the bird with us while he goes on holiday to see his sister in South Africa. He'll be back in three weeks."

"Cool!" Eva grinned. She laughed as Buddy hopped and poppety-popped like crazy in his cage. The talking budgie's bright eyes and tiny sharp claws fascinated her.

"Any post this morning?" Heidi asked as she dashed through Reception.

"Not yet," Eva answered.

"I can't stand this waiting around," her mum sighed. "It's driving me crazy!"

For a while there was a stiff silence. Then Mark abruptly changed the subject. "How's wee Sasha?"

"Good," Eva said with a smile. She'd checked the cute puppy twice already.

"Wee Sasha – 'wee' meaning 'little', not the other…"

Eva raised her eyebrows at the naff joke. "Da-ad! Anyway, why aren't you at work?"

"Day off. And why aren't you at school, Evie-Bee?"

"Summer holidays!" she told him. "As if

you didn't know! And what's with the baby name stuff?"

As they joked around, the main door opened and a tall, fair-haired man and a girl aged about six came in. They glanced round uncertainly, then walked to the desk.

"Can I help?" Mark asked.

Eva noted the small blue pet carrier under the man's arm.

"My name's Francis Nicholls, and this is my daughter Grace. We hope we've come to the right place," the man began.

The little girl looked down at her feet with an unhappy frown.

"This is Animal Magic, where we match the perfect pet with the perfect owner!" Mark announced with a smile. "At least, that's what we try to do."

Mr Nicholls cleared his throat. "Good. Well, I mean, in one way, it's good. But in another way it's not good, is it, Gracie?"

The girl shook her head.

"We're very sorry to part with Bella," her dad went on. He placed the pet carrier on the desk and stood Grace on a chair alongside. "But we're going abroad, so we don't have any choice."

Intrigued, Eva came over to investigate.

"How long will you be away?" Mark asked, thinking that the parting might not be for ever.

"Oh, we're not coming back," Mr Nicholls explained. "We're emigrating to New Zealand. That's why we have to say goodbye to Bella."

"So who's Bella?" Eva asked, carefully unzipping the carrier and peering inside.

At first she saw only a soft, pale-blue blanket. Then, looking more closely, she made out a white shape huddled amongst the folds. It was round and furry, with long ears and enormous dark brown eyes. "A baby rabbit!" she murmured, reaching inside.

But Bella didn't want to be picked up. She turned her back and shrank further into the corner.

"Bella's very shy," Grace's dad explained. "We've only had her for a couple of weeks and we've not been able to coax her out of her shell, I'm afraid."

For the first time Grace spoke up. "She only lets *me* stroke her," she said quietly. "No one else."

Gently the little girl put her hand inside the carrier and stroked Bella's ears.

"Does she take food from your hand?" Eva asked.

Grace nodded. "She likes lettuce and rocket leaves and tiny bits of carrot."

"How come you took Bella on?" Mark asked Francis.

"When we already knew we were emigrating, you mean?"

Mark nodded.

"It was a case of us or nobody, I'm afraid. We found Bella in our garden shed. She was obviously lost. We reckoned she'd given her previous owners the slip, so we took her in and looked after her. My wife put up 'Found' notices around the neighbourhood, but no one came forward to claim her."

Mark nodded and began to take down details. Meanwhile, Grace showed Eva how to stroke Bella.

"You put your hand in front of her, like this. You wait for her to take a sniff. If she likes you, she'll let you move your hand a bit closer, until in the end she lets you stroke her."

Patiently Eva copied Grace. "Poor little Bella!" she sighed. "Don't be shy. I'm not going to hurt you."

The small white rabbit trembled as she sniffed Eva's hand. But she no longer tried to hide in the corner. Instead, she came forward a fraction.

"Lovely girl!" Eva soothed. "You're beautiful, with your big, brown eyes."

Grace nodded and smiled.

Sniff-sniff. Bella's ears twitched as she edged forward.

In the background, Buddy jingled his bell and poppety-popped.

"We live at 23 Riverside Road," Francis told Mark, as he filled in the form. "But we're leaving first thing tomorrow."

"OK, well listen – I'm sure we'll be able

to find Bella a new owner," Mark said, smiling kindly at Grace as her dad helped her down from the chair. "And once she's settled in to her new home, we could send you a message to tell you how happy she is. Would you like us to do that?"

Grace frowned then nodded.

"So we'll email you with the good news. Is that OK?"

Another nod, then Grace blinked back a tear.

"Come on, Gracie, let's go," her dad said briskly. He took her hand. "Say goodbye."

"Goodbye, Bella," Grace whispered as her dad led her away.

Inside the pet carrier, hidden from sight, shy Bella snuggled deep into the blue blanket.

"Where's Neville? Who's a cheeky boy?" Buddy chattered from his perch.

"Let me give you a guided tour of Animal Magic!" Eva said to Bella.

Her mum had run a health check on the baby rabbit and declared her fit. "Very nervous though," she'd warned. "It'll take a while for her to get used to us."

Eva picked up the blue carrier with Bella inside, and made her way to the cattery, which was nice and quiet. "I'm going to read up about rabbit care," she promised, placing the carrier next to a kitten unit and peering in at Bella. "I know you need plenty of clean water to drink, but I want to find out more stuff about a healthy diet and exercise."

Bella sat cosily on her blanket, her white fur fluffy, her ears long and silky.

"This is where we look after cats and kittens," Eva explained, pointing down the row of units. "We've got Bertie and Domino. Domino is the black and white cat. We've already found a home for him. These two kittens are called Missy and Petal."

Though she didn't venture out of her cosy nest, Bella seemed to be paying attention. Her nose twitched and she flicked her long ears.

"Mad!" Karl muttered as he passed through the cattery. "Crazy girl Eva, talking to the animals!"

"And that's my brother, Karl," Eva told Bella. "Ignore everything he says, OK!"

Eva showed Bella the kennels with the noisy dogs, including Billy the bad-boy boxer and Ellie, a calm, sweet-tempered German shepherd.

But shy Bella hid in her dark corner, afraid of the barks and yelps.

So Eva quickly carried her out of the kennels to the small pets section.

"Meet Jimmy," she said to the quivering newcomer. "He's a gorgeous brown and white guinea pig with twinkly pink eyes. And this is Frankie the ferret, who was dumped in a pet shop doorway. He was practically starving. How can people do that? And next to him is Lucky, a Dutch rabbit. I'm sure you'll soon make friends with him."

"Nuts!" Karl commented, coming in to

play with Frankie. He took the ferret from his cage and let him run up his arm on to his shoulder. "Talk, talk, talk to the animals. That's all Eva ever does!"

As usual, Eva ignored her brother and carried on with her guided tour.

"We've got new stables out in the yard. At the moment we don't have anyone living there because it's summer and Guinevere and Merlin stay out in Linda Brooks's field at the back of their house, which is next door."

Bella sniffed the air and edged forward to the door of the carrier. She stared out at her new surroundings.

Frankie ran down Karl's other arm and jumped on to the table beside Bella. A startled Bella cowered back in her dark corner.

"Hey, Frankie, don't scare her!" Eva protested. She knew the ferret was too lively for the shy rabbit. So, with a fresh idea in her head, Eva ran to the kennels to fetch Sasha.

"Now, Sasha, meet Bella. I want you to be nice to Bella. She's new and she needs a friend. I'm relying on you!" Eva introduced the gentle puppy to the young rabbit.

Sasha poked her nose into the carrier and wagged her tail.

"Uh?" Karl quizzed, as Frankie sprinted up and down his arm. "A dog and a rabbit? That's not a good idea."

"Why not?" Eva asked.

"Dog and rabbit together. Dog chases rabbit. Rabbit ends up seriously dead!"

"Not this time." Eva grinned as Sasha made friendly moves towards Bella. "Bella isn't scared – look!"

The white rabbit twitched her ears and sniffed. Her big brown eyes gleamed.

Karl shrugged. "Do what you like," he mumbled. "You always do, anyway."

"They're going to be best mates," Eva promised.

As if to prove it, Sasha crept in beside Bella and snuggled down in the blue blanket.

Things were looking up. Poor, abandoned Sasha was happy. Shy Bella had found a friend.

But even as Eva leaned in and stroked them both, a small worry niggled inside her head.

How come Bella turned up in the Nicholls's garden shed in the first place?

"Where did you come from, you sweet little thing?" she murmured, tickling Bella's ears. "Were you naughty? Did you run away?"

Bella stared up at Eva with her huge, dark eyes.

"Is someone out there still missing you?" Eva wondered aloud. "And if so, how do we find them and take you home?"

Chapter Three

"OK, so *where* is this letter from the Council?" Heidi sighed. She sifted through the mail on the desk in Reception, checking for the third time to see if the letter had arrived.

Joel helped her, while Eva watched Karl enter Bella's details on to the Animal Magic website.

"Bella. Young white rabbit, looking for a friend. Owners have moved away." Karl typed fast then uploaded a picture he had taken with the digital camera. "Is this one OK?" he asked Eva, showing her a close-up of Bella.

She nodded. "So-o cute!"

"I spoke to the man from the Council, Mr Whatisname – Mr Winters – and he insists he sent the letter containing their decision on Monday," Heidi went on. "Of course, he won't tell me what it is over the phone…"

"Is this it?" Joel asked, unearthing a crumpled brown envelope. "Oh no, it's a bill from the builders' yard – for the wood we used to build the stables."

"Don't remind me," Heidi groaned. "It came last month and I still haven't paid it. I'm not likely to be able to find the extra money this month either."

Luckily for Eva, Annie showed up before she got dragged into the search for the Council letter.

"Hey, Eva, when can we take Sasha out?" Annie asked brightly.

"Right now!" Eva jumped at the chance. "Come on, we can start training her too!"

It was a bright, sunny afternoon, and Eva soon forgot the big question mark hanging over the future of Animal Magic.

"The grass is taller than Sasha!" Eva cried as the black puppy scampered through the safely-fenced field at the back of Annie's house. "You can just see the tip of her tail."

Sasha zigzagged through the pink meadow flowers. At the bottom of the field, Guinevere and Merlin grazed quietly.

"Call Sasha back," Annie told Eva. "See if she obeys."

"Here, Sasha!" Eva called.

The puppy romped on, bounding over clumps of buttercups, heading for two women who stood near to the horses.

"That's Mum and Miss Eliot. The old lady called to see Guinevere," Annie reported.

"Here, Sasha!" Eva called more sternly.

Still the puppy scampered on until she reached the horses.

"Oops!" Eva cried, as Guinevere lowered her head and snorted loudly.

Sasha yelped and fled to Linda Brooks for protection. *Save me from that fierce giant with hot breath and enormous hooves!*

Linda picked Sasha up and waited for the girls to join them.

"Sorry, Mrs Brooks, the training isn't going so well!" Eva gasped. "Sasha wouldn't obey my command."

"But she's a cute little thing," the old lady said, reaching out to stroke her.

"Hello, Miss Eliot." Eva smiled at Guinevere's ex-owner. "Isn't Merlin doing well?"

Miss Eliot nodded. "It's lovely to see Guinevere being such a good mother to him. And how are your mother and father getting along with their animal rescue work?"

"Good, thanks," Eva said, carefully avoiding Linda Brooks's gaze as she took Sasha from her. After all, the only cloud on the horizon – the petition to have Animal Magic closed down – had been caused by their next-door neighbour.

Linda blushed but said nothing.

"Come and see us any time you like!" Eva invited.

"I will," Miss Eliot promised with a sweet smile. "In fact, I'd like that very much."

Eva left Annie with her mum and Miss Eliot and ran back home with Sasha. Heidi, Mark and Joel were still searching high and low for the letter from the Council.

"It must be here somewhere," Heidi muttered, down on her hands and knees, looking under the leaflet rack. "It *must* have been delivered by now."

Eva carried Sasha into the small pets section. "What are you doing?" she asked Karl, who was searching inside Jimmy the guinea pig's cage. "Are you still looking for the letter, or did Frankie do a runner again?"

He shook his head and looked worried. "I let Frankie meet Bella – you know, like you did with Sasha – and everything was

OK, they were getting on fine, until I turned my back – just for a second, to get Frankie's food out of the fridge – and when I looked again, well, Bella had vanished!"

"Bella!" Eva echoed. "Where? I mean, how…?"

"I don't know, but she can't have gone far," Karl groaned, peering into Lucky the rabbit's cage. "Eva, we've got to find Bella before Mum finds out. Come on, put Sasha back in her kennel and help me look!"

Chapter Four

Karl and Eva searched every corner of the small pets section.

Eva looked under shelves and inside cupboards. Karl took each animal out of its cage and rooted around in its bedding.

"Any sign?" he asked Eva.

She shook her head. "Mr Nicholls told us Bella was mega timid and that she runs away if anything scares her. I expect that's how she ended up in their shed in the first place."

"Maybe we should try tempting her with some food," Karl suggested.

Eva nodded. "I'll fetch a lettuce leaf."

She opened the fridge door, and reached for the lettuce. "Oh!" she gasped, quickly shutting it again. "Karl, I found Bella!"

Her brother came running. "In the fridge?" he asked.

Eva nodded. "In the veg compartment. She must have snuck in there when you opened the door."

"Phew! Crisis over," Karl said, relieved.

"Yes, but she's going to freeze if she stays in there much longer."

"Yeah, sorry." Karl bit his lip.

"How are we going to get her out?" Eva asked. "If I open the door again, she could jump out and run off. Then we'd be back to where we started."

"Wait, I'll fetch her blue blanket," Karl

decided. "What happens now is that you wait until I've draped this over the fridge, then you open the door again and Bella shoots out, but I've got the blanket blocking her exit and we bundle her up inside it. OK?"

Eva nodded. "It might work," she muttered. In any case, they had to get Bella out of there fast. "Let's give it a go."

Waiting for Karl to get the blanket in position, Eva eased open the fridge door. For a few seconds nothing happened. Then they heard a scrabbling sound and saw a bulge in the blanket as Bella made her bid for freedom.

In a flash Karl let one edge of the blanket drop to trap the baby rabbit inside it. Then Eva picked up the whole bundle and carried it to Bella's pet carrier.

"Good job, Eva!" Karl muttered, very relieved.

Gently Eva released the captive rabbit. Bella sat safe in her carrier, shivering and blinking up at them. "Don't worry, we'll get a proper cage ready for you," Eva murmured, "with cosy bedding and a dish of yummy food."

Bella twitched her long ears and cowered in the corner.

"You can't keep on running away like this," Eva scolded. "You have to learn to let us look after you. After all, it's a big, dangerous world out there for a baby rabbit!"

Bella blinked and seemed to sigh.

"She probably runs away because she's scared," Karl pointed out. "Anyway, I'm going to take Billy for a walk. Let's hope I'm safer with dogs than I am with rabbits!"

"And I'll fix up a cage for Bella," Eva said.

She didn't give Karl a hard time. After all, Bella was back, and that was all that mattered.

"It isn't my day!" Karl said, reappearing five minutes later with Billy the bad-boy boxer. "We didn't get further than Reception."

"What happened?" Eva asked.

She'd found a cage for Bella and finished feeding her. Now she was checking on Jimmy, Lucky and Frankie.

"Billy's been up to his tricks again," Karl groaned. "Anyway, Mum and Dad want you to come over to the house."

Eva washed her hands at the sink. "So what's Billy done this time?" she asked Karl as they dashed through Reception.

"Poppety-poppety-pop!" Buddy croaked. "Where's Neville? Who's a cheeky boy?"

Karl grimaced. "When we got to Reception, Mum and Dad were still looking for that letter."

"From the Council," Eva nodded. "So?"

"So Billy pulls on his lead and drags me to the bench in the waiting area and starts snuffling around underneath it..."

"Don't tell me!" Eva gasped.

Karl nodded. "Underneath is a pile of

well-chewed mail, including the letter from the Council. Billy must have somehow snuck the letters out of the pile of post without anyone seeing him – maybe yesterday or the day before! He's mangled it and dumped it under the bench!"

Eva gave a low whistle.

"So now he remembers where he stashed it, and he goes back and chews it some more – right in front of our eyes!"

"One munched-up piece of precious mail!" Eva gasped.

"Dad managed to rescue the letter before Billy wrecked it completely. They've taken it over to the house. They're waiting for me to fetch you before they open it."

Eva held her breath as they crossed the yard and entered the kitchen. She crossed her fingers, staring at the chewed letter which her mum held in her hands.

"Can I open it now?" Heidi asked Mark. He nodded.

"Let's hope we get the decision we want!" Heidi muttered, opening the letter with trembling fingers.

Chapter Five

"'Dear Mrs Harrison,'" Heidi read slowly.

The edges of the paper were torn and chewed, the middle was scrunched and crumpled.

"'With regard to the matter of the petition raised and presented to the Council by Mrs Linda Brooks of Rose Cottage, Main Street, Okeham...'"

"It's all down to Linda!" Eva muttered to Karl. "None of this would ever have happened if it hadn't been for her!"

"Ssh!" Mark warned, before Heidi read on.

"'After due consideration of all the factors including noise nuisance and change of usage, but mainly the one of frequent traffic access from Main Street into Animal Magic, the Council has decided...'"

"Please, please, please let us stay open!" Eva said softly, her fingers crossed.

Heidi took a breath and glanced up at Mark, "'...to grant permission for the animal rescue centre to remain *open* and to continue its work.'"

"Yes!" Karl jumped up and punched the air. "We can carry on."

"Yes!" Eva sank on to a chair and heaved the biggest sigh of relief. "I can't wait to tell Annie the good news. Hey, and can we have a party to celebrate? Say yes!"

"Good idea," Mark agreed.

He hugged Heidi, who allowed herself ten seconds of glad tears then pulled herself together.

"Sure, we can stay open and that's a big relief," she said. "But at the rate we're going with debts and everything, we're definitely going to have to cut back on

some things. Anyway, it's six o'clock –
time to feed the dogs," she told Karl. "Eva,
will you clean out Buddy's cage, then deal
with the small animals?"

Eva and Karl nodded and shot out of the
house as fast as their legs would carry
them.

"Hey, Billy, you sneaky letter-gobbler –
you're in big trouble!" Karl warned the
boxer.

Billy jumped up and licked Karl's neck.
Then he ran to his bowl and began to wolf
down his supper.

"He is," Karl insisted to Sasha, who
dashed to her kennel door wagging her
tiny black tail. "We need to stop him
eating everything in sight if we're going
to find him a new owner."

Sasha yelped and jumped up at Karl as he brought her bowl.

In his kennel next door, Billy licked the bowl clean.

"Billy's in trouble," Eva told Buddy. She took out the soiled lining from the bottom of his cage and replaced it with a new one.

"Poppety-pop!" Buddy squawked, staring down at Eva's busy hands.

"But I expect Mum will let him off," Eva explained. "The Council said yes to Animal Magic, so she'll be in a mega-good mood! We can stay open, we can stay open!" she trilled. "And Dad says maybe we can have a big party!"

Buddy watched Eva pour seed into his plastic bowl. Fluttering down from his perch, he dipped his head into the bowl and cracked a seed between his beak.

"Of course, we need more kennels," Eva went on happily. She closed the cage door and checked the catch. "We don't have nearly enough space for all the dogs and cats that are brought here."

Going through to the small animals, she chattered on. "Hi, Jimmy, hi, Frankie. Did you hear? The Council will let us stay open!"

Frankie the ferret dived into his deep bed of straw and wood shavings. Jimmy's pink eyes twinkled as he shuffled slowly across his cage.

"Hey, Bella!" Eva said gently to the little white rabbit. "We've just had the best news. Animal Magic can stay open. We can carry on matching the perfect pet with the perfect owner!"

Pausing for thought, Eva gazed at the shy, runaway rabbit. "Don't be scared," she whispered. "We won't send you to a bad home."

Bella twitched her ears and huddled in a tighter ball.

"I promise," Eva insisted, crouching low and meeting Bella's wide, dark gaze. "We'll find someone who loves you and who will look after you really well and will never scare you or make you run away ever again!"

Chapter Six

"Where are we going?" Annie asked Eva.

The two girls cycled along Main Street early on Thursday morning. It was a grey, cloudy day. There were puddles in the road.

"Yuck!" Eva cried as a red car overtook them and splashed her. "I already had my shower this morning, thank you!"

Annie laughed. "So?" she asked. "Where are you dragging me off to this time?"

Eva cycled ahead, turning right at the

top of the main road and heading towards the river. "I've had an idea," was all she would say.

"Where's Eva?" Heidi asked Karl.

Karl was hunched over the computer, trying to set up a visit for Billy. A man called Owen Grey had emailed to say he might be interested in offering him a home.

"Karl, where did Eva go?" Heidi repeated.

"She went out on her bike with Annie," Karl answered.

"Did she say where?"

Karl tapped at the keyboard. "Dunno. She said something about Riverview Road. I'm not sure why."

"What's the big mystery?" Annie insisted as she and Eva leaned their bikes against a bench overlooking the river.

Eva sat her friend down on the bench and talked earnestly. "Listen, I've been thinking a lot about Bella and how shy and nervous she is. She really, really needs a kind owner."

"Not just any stranger who walks into Animal Magic looking for a pet rabbit," Annie agreed.

"I promised I'd find someone who loves her and won't scare her," Eva said.

Annie nodded. "But that still doesn't explain why you dragged me here."

Eva pointed to the row of stone cottages behind them. "This is Riverview Road. The house with the removal van outside is number 23. That's where Grace Nicholls lives."

Annie frowned. "But you told me they were emigrating. That's why Grace had to leave Bella with you."

As the two girls talked, men came and went out of number 23. They carried big packing cases into the van.

"It is," Eva went on. "But Grace cares a lot about Bella. That's why she'll try to help us find the first owners."

"You mean the owners before the Nicholls family?" Annie asked.

"Yes, it just came to me in a flash. We have to find them – trace the clues, track them down – so we can give Bella back to her proper owners!"

"I don't get it," Annie said. "From what you told me, they didn't even bother to try and find her when she ran away."

"Maybe they did, maybe they didn't," Eva argued. "But just because Bella ran off and got lost in the shed, it doesn't mean her owners didn't love her." Trust Annie to squash her brilliant idea!

"But Grace's mum put up notices everywhere."

"I know. But perhaps the owners were away on holiday at the time and never saw them. Who knows?"

As they sat and thought it through, Eva spotted the small, fair-haired figure of Grace Nicholls standing at the gate of number 23. Eva waved then ran to join her.

"How's Bella?" Grace wanted to know, the moment she saw Eva.

"She's fine. She's got a big, comfy cage at Animal Magic. She's nice and warm and she's eating plenty."

Grace nodded slowly. "Is she sad?" she asked, tears welling up in her big grey eyes. "Does she miss me?"

"A little bit," Eva admitted. "But she'll soon settle down. Anyway, I wanted to ask you some more questions about when you found Bella in your shed. Is that OK?"

Slowly Grace nodded, then led Eva into her garden. Annie waited by the removal van.

"Can I see the shed?" Eva asked Grace. "And can you tell me what happened on the day you found Bella?"

"It was busy. We had lots of people

looking round the house," Grace explained as she took Eva round to the shed.

"So when did you find Bella?" she asked.

"After everyone had gone. It was quiet and I was playing by myself in the garden."

"Was the shed door open?"

Grace nodded. "I was playing football and I kicked my ball inside by mistake. I was looking for it under the shelf with all the plant pots, and that's when I found her."

"Was she hiding?"

"Yes. Some plant pots had fallen off the shelf and rolled into a corner. Bella was hiding inside one. She was so scared she was shaking all over."

"I would be too," Eva said quietly. "If I was Bella and I was lost in a big, strange garden with tall trees and dark bushes, I'd be scared stiff. So what did you do?"

"I shut the door, then sat down and talked to her," Grace explained. "I didn't try to pick her up 'cos I didn't want to scare her any more."

Eva smiled at Grace's sweet and serious face. "Then what?"

"After a bit, Bella stopped shivering. She let me stroke her. Then Dad came out looking for me and I asked him to come in and close the shed door. It was Dad who picked Bella up and took her into the house."

"Did she struggle?"

"Yes. She tried to run away from Dad."

"She does that a lot," Eva admitted. "And after that you looked after Bella and she let you be her friend?"

"Yes, and I didn't want to bring her to Animal Magic," Grace sniffed. "I wanted to keep her! But Dad said it was the only thing to do."

The noise of men shifting furniture inside the house reached them, and Eva saw how sad Grace was about leaving Bella. "Bella will be OK, I promise," she told her quietly. "Shall I tell you what I'm planning to do?"

Grace nodded and she wiped a tear from her cheek.

"I want to find the people who lost Bella in the first place. I think they must be sad about her running away and I'm sure they must want her back."

"Are you sure?" Grace whispered. Like Annie, she remembered the notices her mum had put up, and how no one had replied.

"Certain!" Eva said with a bright smile. "And when I find her real owners, I'll email and tell you. I'll even send you a lovely picture of Bella with her family, back where she belongs!"

Chapter Seven

"My mum says you should never make promises you can't keep," Annie told Eva.

All the way back home from Riverview Road, Annie had been grumbling about Eva's brilliant idea.

"Who says I can't keep my promise?" Eva retorted. "I reckon it can't be too hard to track down Bella's proper owner."

"And if your cunning plan works, what then?" At the gate of Animal Magic, Annie braked then got off her bike. "Like I said –

I really don't think the person who lost Bella cares about her, otherwise they'd have tried really hard to find her after she'd run away."

Eva got off her bike and looked Annie in the eye. "Sometimes you're so…"

"…So?"

"…So *annoying*!" Eva replied, flouncing off across the yard.

"Billy's really friendly and good-natured," Karl was telling Owen Grey in Reception.

Owen had driven out from town especially to see the boxer. He nodded and stroked the dog, who wriggled his backside and wagged his tail.

"He likes you," Karl said.

Behind the desk, Heidi and Joel worked at the computer, updating their records.

"I had a boxer called Lennox when I was a kid," Owen told them. "I've always liked this breed."

"Then you know they need plenty of exercise," Heidi warned.

Karl frowned. He could see that Owen and Billy were bonding like crazy and secretly hoped that his mum wouldn't come out with the stuff about Billy's bad chewing habit.

"I don't mind that," Owen said. "Walking Billy would get me out of the house. But how come he ended up here with you?"

"His previous owners had little kids. They couldn't cope," Karl said vaguely. Out of the corner of his eye he saw Eva flounce through the main door and head straight for one of the computers.

"Actually, Billy has one very bad habit," Heidi told Owen.

Uh-oh! Inwardly Karl groaned. That was it – they might as well take an ugly mug-shot of Billy and put him permanently behind bars!

"He chews," Heidi explained. "Shoes, furniture – anything he can get his teeth into. We have to warn you in advance, because there would be no point in you taking him home and finding out the hard way."

"Oh yeah, I remember Lennox used to do that," Owen said, thoughtfully patting Billy's broad head. "He wrecked three pairs of my dad's slippers, but my mum cured him in the end."

"How?" Karl asked quickly.

Owen shook his head. "Don't know. I can't remember. I'll have to ask Mum."

"Well, we'd love to know how to cure him," Heidi said, smiling.

Owen nodded. "But listen, now you've told me about this, I'll definitely need a day or two to think about adopting Billy. And I need to discuss it with my girlfriend – OK?"

"Fine," Heidi agreed.

Not fine! Karl thought. *It's back to the kennels for you, Billy boy!*

As he led Billy out of Reception, he glanced over Eva's shoulders and saw her tapping away at the keyboard. "Do you know this rabbit?" he read in large letters on the screen. Underneath was a big photo of Bella. "What are you up to?" he mumbled.

"What does it look like? I'm writing a leaflet."

Billy had stopped and turned to see Owen Grey leave the building without looking back. He whined and sidled close to Karl.

"A leaflet? What for?" Karl asked.

"To put through people's letter boxes." Eva concentrated on her typing. "Bella is a runaway rabbit who misses her owners. If you recognize her, please email us at animalmagicrescue@lineone.net."

"The Nicholls already tried that," Karl pointed out.

"No they didn't. They only put up posters. They didn't deliver them to people's houses."

"Did you check with Mum and Dad?"

"Nope. But don't worry, they'll say it's a good idea." Eva was confident that her parents would back her up.

"Anyway, how do you know Bella's first owners weren't cruel to her? Maybe that's why she ran away in the first place," Karl pointed out.

Eva sighed. "Listen!" she said. "I don't know for sure, do I? But my guess is they were nice, kind people. They were just careless for a moment and let Bella escape. Now they're really sad that she's missing."

"Says you!" Karl retorted. He still wasn't convinced. "Anyway, posting leaflets through doors won't do any good."

"Shut up, Karl!" Eva snapped. She clicked the print key and waited for the leaflets to roll out of the printer.

"We've got three enquiries from people interested in adopting Sasha," Heidi reported to Eva when she came back from delivering Bella leaflets up and down Main Street.

"Cool," Eva muttered. She tweeted at Buddy in his cage behind Reception, then placed her spare leaflets on the desk.

"Do you want to help with a vaccination?" her mum asked, looking towards the entrance at a man and a boy with a small black and white puppy. "Hello, Mr Goodall, hello, Ben!" she called. "Come right this way."

Eva nodded and went into the surgery where she cleaned the table with antiseptic spray. Then Ben and his dad brought the puppy in and Heidi followed.

"Thanks for fitting us in so quickly," Mr Goodall told her. "I've been telling Ben that we can't take Bertie for walks until he's been vaccinated."

"Quite right," Heidi nodded. "How old is Bertie? About seven weeks?"

"Six and a half," Mr Goodall confirmed. "We bought him from a dubious place, I'm afraid. The mother is a pure-bred Lab, and the owners were trying to fob this little chap off as pure Labrador too, but I could tell at a glance that he wasn't. My bet is, there's a fair bit of Border collie in him too."

Heidi glanced at Eva. "Sounds like Bertie comes from the same litter as Sasha – a cross-breed puppy who was brought in to us a couple of days ago. I hope you didn't pay a pedigree price."

"No," Mr Goodall replied, as Heidi quickly gave Bertie his jab and gave him back to Ben. "We're moving out to Okeham from the city, which is finally why we allowed Ben to have a puppy."

As her mum lead Ben and his dad back into Reception, Eva slipped off to see Bella.

"I saw Grace," she murmured, putting her nose against the front of Bella's cage.

"She's missing you loads."

Bella twitched her nose and took one short hop towards Eva.

"I'm going to post leaflets about you through every letter box in the village," Eva went on. "I've already started on Main Street."

Another hop closer. Bella seemed less shy today, perhaps drawn by the sound of Eva's gentle voice.

"This is good. You like me talking to you, don't you?" Eva said.

But suddenly Bella's ears twitched and she shot back into the darkest corner. She'd caught sight of a face at the window.

Eva glanced round in time to see Ben Goodall peering in at them. He looked flushed, and his forehead was creased in a worried frown.

Thanks, Ben! Eva thought. *Just when I was getting to bond with Bella you have to go and startle her!*

Ben saw Eva watching him and quickly ducked out of sight.

Weird! Eva said to herself. *Why is he acting so strange?*

In the corner of her cage, Bella sat huddled into a soft white ball, with only her big dark eyes moving, looking out for enemies and trying to hide.

"I'll come and talk to you later," Eva sighed. With shy Bella, it was always one step forwards and two steps back.

Chapter Eight

Early next morning Eva went out to deliver more of her Bella leaflets.

"Good luck!" Mark shouted from his van as he set off for work. He and Eva had discussed her plan to find Bella's real owner and, unlike Karl, he'd thought the leaflets were a good idea.

"Thanks, Dad!" Eva smiled and waved.

She headed down Main Street, turning into Chestnut Crescent and pushing a leaflet through the letter box of each neat bungalow. Back on Main Street, she came to Swallow Court, and wasn't surprised to see Miss Eliot standing at the door of her small bungalow. She waved at the old lady and went across.

"Have you seen Tigger?" Miss Eliot asked.

Tigger was Miss Eliot's beloved tabby cat. Eva shook her head.

"I'm worried about the traffic. Tigger isn't used to it."

"Don't worry, I'll keep a lookout. Would you like one of these?" Eva showed the old lady her leaflet.

Miss Eliot nodded. "I hope you succeed in finding the owner. She's such a sweet little rabbit, isn't she? Someone somewhere must be heartbroken about losing her."

"That's exactly what I think!" Eva agreed.

"And how is your mother? And the rescue centre?"

"Cool, actually. The Council says we can stay open, which is a great big weight off our shoulders. But it means Mum is mega busy. Besides, she's worried about owing people money. But that doesn't stop you popping in to see us any time you want, by the way," Eva gabbled. She liked Miss Eliot, but she was eager to get on her way.

"I must bring Tigger in soon for her flu jab," the old lady said, relieved when she spotted the little tabby strolling across the lawn in the centre of the courtyard. "Here, Tigger!" she called and clapped her hands.

Seizing her chance, Eva hurried on. Soon she'd made it to the edge of the village, so she crossed the road, turned into a side street and delivered her leaflets to the big houses on Earlswood Avenue.

"Hey, Eva!" Karl's friend, George Stevens, was in his driveway, dressed in jeans and a blue T-shirt, his dark hair tousled as if he'd just crawled out of bed. "What have you got there?"

"Leaflets." Eva blushed and tried to squeeze past. Somehow George always made her feel about five years old. He acted like he was a grown-up, looking down at a snotty-nosed kid.

"Show!" George stretched out his hand and snatched a leaflet. "Hmm, cute. Is this the rabbit Karl told me about – the one that ran off and hid in the fridge?"

Eva nodded, her cheeks flushing deeper than ever.

"As it happens, we've got a spare rabbit cage and a run in our back garden," George went on. "I kept rabbits when I was younger, but I haven't had one for a while. I like the look of Bella though."

"Right," Eva muttered. "But actually, Bella's different. We're not trying to find a new home for her right now."

"Are you sure? Karl said he'd put her on the website."

Eva swallowed hard. "Yeah, but look at the leaflet. It says that we're searching for Bella's proper owner."

"That's not what Karl told me." George frowned. "I bet if I went down to Animal Magic right now and offered five-star rabbit accommodation in a big cage with a long run out the back your mum would snap my hand off!"

"I don't think so." Eva shook her head. "That's not the plan for Bella."

But the more she argued, and the longer George looked at Bella's cute photo, the less he seemed to be listening.

"In fact, I think I'll cycle down there right now," George decided, disappearing inside the garage to fetch his bike.

"No – wait!" Eva said feebly. She had to step quickly out of George's way as he set off down the drive. "I promised Grace Nicholls ... we need to find out who Bella really belongs to... Don't, George. Please listen to me!"

But he was gone, and Eva was left with a bunch of leaflets and a sinking feeling that Bella's future had suddenly slipped out of her hands.

"What's got into you? You should be pleased!" Karl stood behind the desk in Reception, ready for a face-off with Eva.

George had beaten her back to Animal Magic and had already put in his offer to give Bella a new home. He appealed to Heidi, who was studying spreadsheets on the computer. "We've got the hutch and everything. You can come and see it if you want."

"But, Mum, can't we wait a few days?" Eva pleaded. She was wishing desperately that she'd found time to talk to her mum about her plan. "Does Bella have to be re-homed right away?"

Karl stepped in on his friend's side. "Course she does! Mum, don't listen to Eva. Bella would love it at George's place. And he's had pet rabbits before, remember!"

"I promised Grace I'd find Bella's real owner!" Eva told her mum. "Dad knows about it. And Bella's really shy and scared. She needs someone special."

"Hey, watch it," Karl muttered. "Are you saying George isn't special?"

"No. I didn't mean that." Eva grew flustered. "It's just too soon. Bella needs to stay here for a while."

"Make your mind up," Karl snapped. "One minute you want to send her back to an owner who let her run off in the first place and couldn't care less about her anyway. The next minute, you want to keep her here!"

Sighing, Heidi broke off from her work. "Karl – Eva, stop arguing. It's giving me a headache."

Karl clamped his mouth shut and frowned at Eva. She took a deep breath and glared back.

"That's better." Heidi came to the counter to talk to George. "It's good of you to offer Bella a home," she began.

Yesss! Karl stared triumphantly at his sister.

"But have you checked it out with your mum and dad?"

Course he hasn't! Eva gritted her teeth and carried on glaring. *He got on his bike and dashed straight down here!*

"Mum won't mind," George answered steadily.

"But you haven't actually asked her yet?"

"No."

See! Eva outstared her brother.

Karl dropped his gaze and shuffled some papers on the counter.

"What I suggest is this," Heidi decided, turning to Eva and trying to soften the blow. "We have to be sensible about it.

I think George should go home and talk to his parents about offering Bella a home. If they say yes, we should go ahead because we know George and we can be sure that he'll take good care of Bella."

So who's in the right now? Karl flashed Eva a final look of triumph.

Eva's heart thudded. Her shoulders sagged.

"But!" Heidi held up a warning finger. "In the meantime, Eva, I suggest you carry on with your search."

Eva took a sharp breath then nodded.

"Let's give you twenty-four hours to find Bella's first owner. If by then you haven't succeeded, and if George's parents agree, we'll rehome her at Earlswood Avenue – end of story!"

Chapter Nine

Never make a promise you can't keep! Annie's words ran through Eva's head as she went out to deliver more leaflets.

She thought of Grace Nicholls and her parents packing up all their stuff and moving away to New Zealand, and she worried about poor little Bella cowering in her cage and hiding from the world.

She had a day to try to keep her promise and about twenty more houses in the village to deliver to. With every click of a letter box, she prayed that the mystery of Bella's real owner would be solved.

"OK?" Heidi asked when Eva at last walked back into the kitchen. It was one o'clock – time for a quick break from the busy routine at Animal Magic.

"I suppose." Eva nodded.

"No luck with Bella's original owners, I take it?"

A quick shake of the head was all Eva could manage.

"Well, look at it this way," Heidi went on cheerfully. "If Bella is rehomed with George, at least you and Karl will be able to pop in and visit her as often as you like."

"Mum, I don't want to talk about it," Eva muttered, glancing out of the kitchen window and seeing Ben Goodall carrying Bertie across the yard. "Is Joel in Reception?" she checked.

"I'm not sure, but you can go and see," Heidi replied.

Eva sped across the yard and caught up with Ben. "What's up with Bertie?" she asked as she held the door open and they went inside to find Joel manning the desk.

"He's not eating properly," Ben told her. "I tried him with puppy food, but he wasn't interested."

"Let me take a look at him," Joel offered.

Little Bertie squirmed then wagged his tail at Joel.

"He seems lively enough. Let's take his temperature and check him over... Yep, quite normal."

Eva watched Ben Goodall closely. The boy's attention didn't seem to be on Bertie at all, she noticed. Instead, he sifted through the leaflets on the desk.

"Can I help?" she offered.

"No. Yes. Erm, have you got a leaflet on feeding puppies?" he mumbled.

Eva got him one from the rack.

"His temperature's normal and there's no tenderness around his stomach," Joel reported. "Maybe Bertie is having a slight reaction to the jab we gave him, that's all."

Ben nodded. "Oh, and have you got one of those leaflets about the runaway rabbit?" he dropped in casually. But his face was bright red and his eyes were worried.

"No, sorry, I posted the last ones earlier this morning." *Wait a minute!* Eva thought. *Why are you so interested in Bella? How come you snuck a look at her through the window yesterday when you thought no one would be watching?*

Ben frowned and mumbled. "OK, no problem."

"While you're here, let me finish putting Bertie's information on file," Joel suggested, turning to the computer. "We must have been too busy yesterday to take everything down."

"Age – six and a half weeks, which means Bertie was born…"

"What do you know about Bella?" Eva hissed at Ben. This time she wasn't going to let him sneak away.

"Nothing!" he said quickly. "I don't know anything!"

"Are you sure?" Eva didn't believe him. He'd answered too quickly and refused to meet her gaze.

"I said, nothing – OK!" Sulkily Ben picked Bertie up and made as if to leave.

But Joel had one more question. "Hang on a sec, Ben – where do you live? We didn't take down your address."

"We live on Riverview Road," Ben answered in his usual mumble. "We've just moved in."

"Riverview Road," Joel typed on the keyboard. "What number?"

"Number 23," Ben told him, escaping through the door as fast as he could.

Eva stood for a few moments gawping at the door.

"What is it?" Joel asked. "You look like you've seen a ghost."

"23 Riverview Road," Eva repeated under her breath. "That's where Grace Nicholls lived. The Goodalls must have moved into her house!"

"So?" Joel didn't get the point. He scratched his head and stared after Eva as she charged after Ben and overtook him at the gate.

"Wait!" she yelled.

"Leave me alone," Ben said. He brushed past Eva. "I don't want to talk to you."

"That's because you're feeling guilty," Eva guessed. "You're acting weird because of Bella, aren't you?"

"No. Go away." Ben marched up Main Street with Bertie on his lead. "I don't know what you're talking about."

"Stop!" Eva ran in front of Ben and blocked his way. "I can't quite make sense of this yet, but I've got a feeling that Bella belongs to you!"

Ben came to a sudden halt. "Don't be stupid," he argued feebly. "We only just moved in to our new house."

"So you've never seen Bella before?"

He quickly shook his head and tried to barge past once more. But Eva stood her ground.

"Then how come you snuck a look at her yesterday. And why did you want a leaflet?" Eva ran through her list of suspicions. "Last of all, why pretend Bertie was ill and bring him into Animal Magic?"

"I wasn't pretending," Ben faltered. Then he changed his mind. "OK then, what if I was?"

Eva stared at him long and hard. "You're either very weird, or you know something you're not telling," she accused.

Ben had run out of arguments. "What if I do?" he said huffily. "It's none of your business."

Eva seized her chance. "It is my business," she insisted.

"Right, OK, Miss Clever! How would you feel if you had a pet and you did something you shouldn't, and it meant that everything went wrong and you didn't know any way of putting it right?"

"Slow down!" Eva begged. "What did you do?"

"If I tell you, you mustn't tell anybody else!" Ben pleaded.

Eva nodded. "I won't."

"Mum and Dad gave me a pet rabbit when we lived at our old house on Cannon Street, in town."

"It's near where I go to school," Eva said quickly.

"I hadn't had her very long. I called her Maisie. She was only a baby and I hated leaving her on her own. And what I did, which I should never have done, was to sneak her into my dad's car one day without my parents knowing."

"Why?" Eva wanted to know.

"Because I thought she'd be lonely if I left her behind in her hutch and I knew Mum and Dad would say no if I asked if we could bring her along."

"OK. Then what?"

"Then my dad drove us out here to Okeham to see the house we were moving to," Ben explained.

"Number 23 Riverview Road!"

"Right," Ben said glumly. "Anyway, Mum and Dad went into the house to measure windows for curtains and stuff, and I stayed in the car with Maisie. I was playing with her and I didn't notice Mum and Dad come back."

"So Maisie was loose in the car?" Eva prompted.

Ben nodded. "Mum opened the car door and frightened Maisie and she jumped out, but Mum was too busy to notice."

"Maisie ran away?"

"Yes. And I couldn't get out and chase her because I wasn't supposed to have her with me in the first place. Anyway, before I knew it, Dad had started the car and we were on our way."

"Then it was too late." Eva got a clear

picture of what had happened. "And when you got back home, your mum and dad found the hutch was empty and believed Maisie had escaped from your garden in Cannon Street. You went along with it, so as not to get into trouble?"

Miserably, Ben nodded again. "Yes, what else could I do? But then we moved here and yesterday I saw those rabbit leaflets on your counter."

"And now you want to know if Bella is the same rabbit as the one you lost?" Eva asked, her eyes sparkling eagerly.

"Yeah. I mean, could it be Maisie? She looks the same."

"And she's a runaway. She was found in the garden shed at number 23." The story fitted. Eva held her breath.

"I never knew that. So you think there's a good chance?" Ben asked.

"That Maisie is Bella? Yes, I do!" She felt sorry and nervous – sorry for Ben, who had got himself into this mess, and nervous in case she was wrong. "Come on," she said, turning Ben and Bertie around and heading back to Animal Magic. "There's only one way to find out. Let's go and take a closer look!"

Chapter Ten

"Owen Grey said yes!" Karl stood in the rescue centre doorway with bad-boy Billy. He greeted Eva and Ben with a broad smile. "I talked to him on the phone. His girlfriend says yes, he can adopt Billy."

"Great news!" Eva said. She patted Billy, who wagged his stumpy tail.

"Owen's mum says she'll train Billy out of chewing stuff he shouldn't," Karl went on. "She did it once before with Lennox, so she reckons she can do it again."

"Sounds perfect," Eva said, hurrying on with Ben and Bertie.

"Poppety-pop! Where's Neville?" Buddy the budgie chirped from his perch.

"And we've got a woman called Emma Dibb coming in to see Sasha this afternoon," Joel reported from his seat at the computer. "She already owns a brown Labrador and she lives in a house overlooking a park where she can walk the dog, so she sounds promising."

"Good. Cool. Great," Eva gabbled. "Come on, Ben, what are you waiting for?"

Ben hung back in Reception. "I-I've changed my mind," Ben stammered.

Eva's jaw dropped. She noticed that Joel was watching Ben closely, as if he was about to step in and say something.

So she grabbed Ben by the arm and marched him through the door into the small animals unit. "Are you crazy?" she hissed. "You can't change your mind about stuff as important as this!"

Ben shook his head. "I'm going to be in big trouble with Mum and Dad if they find out," he muttered. "I mean, if Bella turns out to be Maisie like you think – well, what am I going to tell them?"

Eva studied his frowning face. "Try the truth," she said matter-of-factly. "Tell them you made a mistake."

Leaving Ben to work through his problem, she approached Bella's cage. "Hi there!" she murmured to the shy creature huddled in the folds of her favourite blue blanket. "Someone's come to see you!"

Warily, Bella edged forward, responding as usual to Eva's gentle voice. She twitched her soft pink nose and flicked her ears.

"I think you'll remember this person," Eva whispered. Slowly she opened the cage door and let Bella sniff her hand. Then gently she picked her up and lifted her out.

Ben stared at Eva and Bella. His frown disappeared and he came closer. "It's Maisie!" he said, unable to take his eyes off the tiny rabbit. "Definitely her. I'm totally sure!"

"I knew it was," Eva smiled.

The baby rabbit snuggled close against her, blinking her big dark eyes.

"Can I hold her?" Ben asked.

"Of course you can – she's your rabbit!" Taking Bertie from Ben, she handed Bella over.

"Hey, Maisie!" Ben whispered, his eyes filling with tears. "It's me – Ben!"

The rabbit sniffed his hand and T-shirt. She didn't struggle or try to hide.

"She remembers you!" Eva told him. "She's not the least bit shy."

"I can't believe it," Ben murmured, holding his pet rabbit close to his chest. Then he took a big decision. "Don't worry, Maisie – whatever Mum and Dad say, I'm never going to let you go ever again!"

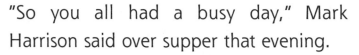

"So you all had a busy day," Mark Harrison said over supper that evening.

"Karl successfully rehomed Billy," Heidi reported. "Joel thinks he found a new owner for Sasha, and George Stevens agreed to take Lucky, the black and white Dutch rabbit."

"Huh?" Mark paused, fork in hand. "When I spoke to you earlier, didn't you say that George wanted to offer a home to the little white one – what's her name?"

"Bella," Karl told him.

"Maisie!" Eva cut in. "Her real name's Maisie, and we did what I wanted to do – we found her first owner!"

"Not so much of the 'we'," Karl corrected. "Eva went solo on this one." He tried to sound casual, but secretly he was well impressed with his little sister.

"Eva did really well," Heidi said with a smile. "The way she tracked down all the clues, I'm convinced she's going to be a private detective when she's older!"

Eva glowed with pride. "The real owner's name is Ben Goodall," she told her dad. "He lives at the Nicholls's old house. It's a long story."

"Lo-ong!" Karl broke in with a pantomime yawn. "So, Dad, you want to know how come George took Lucky?" he asked Mark.

"I've a feeling you're going to tell me."

"OK, so he comes to Animal Magic with his mum to say, yes they can give Bella a home. They arrive at the same time as Mr Goodall. It turns out Joel has phoned him and asked him to come across to Animal Magic."

"Because Joel was worried about Ben coming in with Bertie when there was obviously nothing wrong with the puppy," Eva cut in. This was her story and she wanted to tell it her way. "So Ben walks out of the small pets section with Bella, whose real name is Maisie, like I said. He sees his dad and he's shaking from head to foot."

"But it turns out Mr Goodall is happy that Ben found his pet rabbit at long last,"

Karl explained. "And when he finds out the whole truth, he doesn't throw a wobbler, like Ben expected."

"Whoa!" Mark put up his hands to ward off the flood of facts. "I take it that's why George offered *Lucky* a home – because Bella, whose real name is Maisie, had been reunited with Ben?"

Karl and Eva nodded.

"You should've seen Ben's face when I first handed Maisie over to him," Eva sighed. "He was so-o-o happy!"

"And Mr Goodall said he'd buy a hutch before the pet shop in town closed, and Ben could take his long-lost baby rabbit away right then and there," Karl said. He polished off his plate of fish pie. "Happy ending. Then Eva nearly goes and spoils it all by blubbing."

"I never did!" Eva objected. Sure, she'd

been sorry to say goodbye to Bella and there had been tears in her eyes, but mainly she was happy for Bella – and Lucky – and Billy – and Sasha! Everything had worked out. "We had such a cool day!" she sighed.

"Dear Grace," Eva wrote in her email. *"This is a picture of Bella in her new hutch. And guess what? She's living with Ben Goodall at your old house."*

Clicking the mouse to move Bella's image on to an email attachment, Eva blew the image up to fill the screen.

Bella–Maisie had been staring right at the camera when Eva took the shot. The photo had captured all of her best points – her little round face, her furry body and those long silky soft ears.

"Cute!" she breathed.

"Bella is back where she belongs like I promised," Eva wrote to Grace. *"What do you think? How cool is that!"*

Collect all the books in the
Animal Rescue series!

The unwanted puppy

When Eva finds Honey, a beautiful golden retriever puppy, dumped on the doorstep of Animal Magic, she's desperate to find the lovable dog a new home. But Karl has other ideas... he wants to follow up the clue to find Honey's real owner...

The home-alone kitten

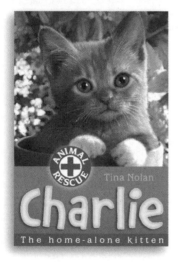

When soccer star Jake Adams cancels his appearance at Animal Magic's Open Day, Eva's determined to find out why. But when she and Karl arrive at Jake's house, all they find is his ginger kitten, Charlie, locked out and miaowing on the doorstep...

Merlin

The homeless foal

When Merlin the foal is born at Animal Magic, Eva is desperate for him to be re-homed nearby, but it seems as if he will be moved to a farm too far away to visit. And that's not all Eva has to worry about: Mrs Brooks's plans to close down the rescue centre look set to become a reality...

Rusty

The injured fox cub

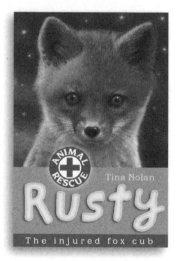

When Eva discovers an injured fox cub down by the river she's desperate to help nurse him back to health. Rusty's gorgeous – he's so small and soft, with golden brown eyes and big pointed ears. Eva can't help picking him up and cuddling him, but will her love ruin Rusty's chances of being returned to the wild?

And look out for the next
book in the series
coming soon!

The lost duckling